Protected by th...
A story of patriotism

WRITTEN BY TRAVIS VELAZQUEZ
ILLUSTRATED BY SUZANNE SHEDOSKY

Today in the news the war is still going strong.

Some people have been saved and others are gone.

The fighting persists as the enemy moves back

Because the U.S. Army is still on the attack!

Travis turns to his Mom and Dad

And says, "This is terribly sad!

How can I help a soldier in need?

There has to be a way to help them succeed!"

Dad says, "Son, that's very kind of you;

_I do_ know a way you can help out our troops!

You can send them a letter to show them you care,

And make them feel better since _they_ can't be _here!_

Travis ran to his room to grab a pen and paper,

An envelope, scissors , pencil and eraser.

He wrote a nice letter and then sealed it himself.

Then put on the stamp that he found on the shelf.

4

Dad walks Travis to the blue mailbox a few block's away,

So he could send his letter and make a soldier's day!

Smiling ear to ear, Travis was full of delight-

So much so, he probably wouldn't sleep tonight.

While they were walking, they saw a group in a huddle,

Yelling and stepping on our flag in a puddle.

"What are they doing, and why would they step on the flag?"

"They're free to express their rights son, even if it makes us sad."

6

"How can we help our flag? This doesn't seem right!"

Just then, the group walked off out of sight.

Dad picked up the flag; it was torn and tattered.

"They did a number on old glory son; she's badly battered."

He folded her up and held her in his hand.

"Never disgrace our flag son; she represents our land.

She is a symbol of how we've grown as a nation,

Even if we hear otherwise from the TV station."

The next block down, they see a man asking for change.

"What's wrong with that guy Dad? He seems strange.

He has patches on his shirt like a police officer would wear."

"That's a _veteran_ son. _He's_ fought for our country here and there.

Those patches represent where he has been,

And what he has done with all of his men.

That metal bracelet he wears around his wrist

Reminds him of his friends he has laid to rest.

We can give him a few dollars for some warm food.

That should help put him in a _positive_ mood!"

The third block down, they found a mailbox to drop the letter inside.

Travis looked at his father, then looked to the ground, and sighed...

"What's wrong son? Why do you look so down?"

"I feel like I didn't do enough, and the soldiers will frown.

I feel like they deserve much more than my _little_ letter.

That's why I'm upset. I want _their_ life to be better."

"Son, it's not about how much you wrote with your pen.

Those soldiers will be happy that you remembered them!

Soldiers don't defend our country to become rich and famous.

They want us to live a free life that they fought to give us."

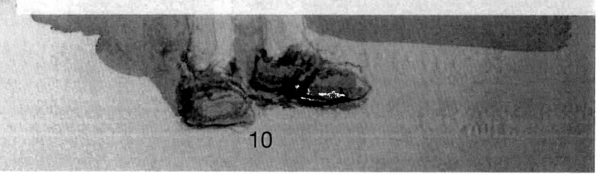

Travis started feeling better as he began to walk back home with Dad.

When suddenly, BOOM! The sky lit up bright, and it made him feel sad,

And scared, and not safe as he trembled with fear!

"Don't be scared son, they are fireworks for today's cheer!

Today is the Fourth of July and we celebrate our independence.

So they light up the sky for our remembrance

For those who have fallen and will never return

Because those men and women have families that yearn."

"We show the whole country that we've not forgotten

About the ones who came back in a flag-draped coffin.

And even though not everything here is perfectly bliss,

We will withstand and overcome all of this.

Our country gets stronger and stronger each year

Because we do not display cowardice or fear!

We look our enemies straight in the eyes

And never back down no matter its size!

Travis finally got home and ran up the stairs

To tell his mother of the day's affairs!

Outside, dad unfolded the flag from his hand

And raised the flag, on his flag pole stand.

He stepped back and gave old glory one big salute

As a tear dropped down from his eye to his boot.

Dad went upstairs to find his son almost asleep.

"Tell me more Dad! I promise to not make a peep!"

12

"Son, one day our country may call upon you

To protect the almighty red, white, and blue.

And one day you will have a boy or girl just like me,

And you will want them to live in the land of the free.

So you may, one day, have to answer that call

To defend the greatest country of all.

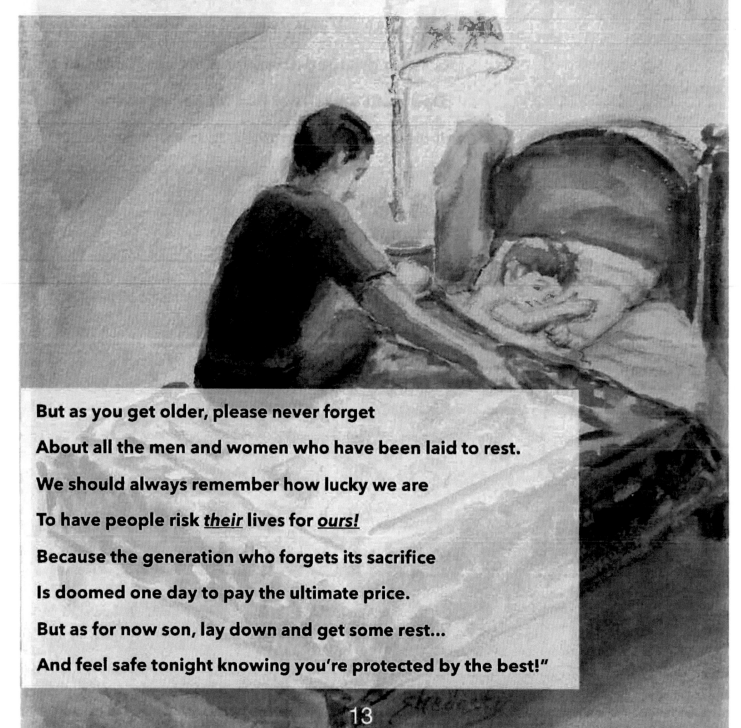

But as you get older, please never forget

About all the men and women who have been laid to rest.

We should always remember how lucky we are

To have people risk _their_ lives for _ours!_

Because the generation who forgets its sacrifice

Is doomed one day to pay the ultimate price.

But as for now son, lay down and get some rest...

And feel safe tonight knowing you're protected by the best!"

The End

"For those who have fought for it, life has a special flavor the protected will never know."

-Master Sergeant Roy Benavidez

Dedication

This book is dedicated to all the men and women who are no longer here to read bedtime stories to their children. Their ultimate sacrifice will never be forgotten. A specific acknowledgement to Elvis Bourdon, Anthony Venetz, and Jose Montenegro all KIA, and all of those who served in the military with the author.

*This book contains 22 pages to represent the 22 veterans that are no longer with us daily due to the struggles of war. Thank a veteran in your own special way, and teach your children to do the same!

About the Author

Travis Velazquez is a proud Army and Air Force Veteran. In the Army, Travis was an infantry soldier with the 4th Infantry Division in Fort Hood Texas. With the Air Force Reserves, Travis was with the 440th Airlift Wing from Milwaukee, Wisconsin (no longer in service). He is currently a real estate agent in Sycamore, Illinois. Travis is married to his wife Evangeline and together they have three wonderful children (in order of photo): Travis, Alejandra, and Bradley. Travis made this book as a remembrance to his fellow brothers in arms who lost their lives on foreign soil. He is an avid supporter of our military. He hopes that this book will help instill pride in our military amongst our children. Travis can be reached at: **realtor_travis@yahoo.com, use subject: Protected by the Best**

About the Illustrator

Suzanne Shedosky is an artist in rural Prophetstown, Illinois. Sue has multiple family members that served in the military including her brother and many family members throughout the years that served as far back as the Korean War, Vietnam War, and World War 2. When Sue was asked to illustrate this book, she gladly accepted and believes whole heartedly in the message the book offers young people of our Nation. Sue is an award winning artist with such awards as the "Best of Show" in Chicago, Illinois and the "Silver Medal of Honor for Oil" in New York City, New York. Sue can be reached at: **shedoskyart@gmail.com**

** A special thank you to Tom & Andrea Davies, Judith Brady, Roger Godinez and Evangeline Velazquez. Your creativity and assistance made this book possible. I also want to thank my kids. They inspire me everyday to become a better person. Thank you!

If you could thank a soldier, what would you tell him or her?

Protected by the best - A story about patriotism
Written by Travis Velazquez

Protected by the best - A story about patriotism
Written by Travis Velazquez

Draw a picture for a soldier!

Protected by the best - A story about patriotism
Written by Travis Velazquez

If you would like to write a letter to a military servicemen, please tear off the last page and send to:

A Million Thanks
17853 Santiago Blvd, #107-355
Villa Park, CA 92861

When you receive a letter, add a photo on social media with the hashtag:

#protectedbythebest

to see other children who have made a soldiers day!

If you wish to donate toys to families of fallen soldiers, please visit:

www.asoldierschild.org

Made in the USA
Lexington, KY
07 November 2018